Heartsong and the Best Bridesmaids

Daisy Meadows

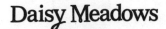

ORCHARD

Rotherham Libraries	
B55 074 215 X	
PETERS	21-Dec-2021
	6.99
CHILD	RTCLS

First published in Great Britain in 2021 by The Watts Publishing Group

3 5 7 9 10 8 6 4 2

Text copyright © 2021 Working Partners Limited
Illustrations © Orchard Books 2021
Series created by Working Partners Limited

The moral rights of the author and illustrator have been asserted. All characters and events in this publication, other than those clearly in the public domain, are fictitious and any resemblance to real persons, living or dead, is purely coincidental.

All rights reserved.
No part of this publication may be reproduced, stored in a retrieval system, or transmitted, in any form or by any means, without the prior permission in writing of the publisher, nor be otherwise circulated in any form of binding or cover other than that in which it is published and without a similar condition including this condition being imposed on the subsequent purchaser.

A CIP catalogue record for this book is available from the British Library.

ISBN 978 1 40836 394 2

Printed and bound in Great Britain by Clays Ltd, Elcograf S.p.A.

The paper and board used in this book are made from wood from responsible sources.

Orchard Books
An imprint of Hachette Children's Group
Part of The Watts Publishing Group Limited
Carmelite House
50 Victoria Embankment
London EC4Y 0DZ

An Hachette UK Company
www.hachette.co.uk
www.hachettechildrens.co.uk

Heartsong and the Best Bridesmaids

Daisy Meadows

ORCHARD

Contents

Story One
A Giant Celebration

Story Two
A Family Fail

Story Three
True Love Conquers All

Meet the Characters

Aisha and Emily are best friends from Spellford Village. Aisha loves sports, whilst Emily's favourite thing is science. But what both girls enjoy more than anything is visiting Enchanted Valley and helping their unicorn friends, who live there.

Heartsong

Heartsong is in charge of weddings in Enchanted Valley. Her three lockets make sure that married couples enjoy true love, and that wedding celebrations are truly magical.

Selena is a wicked unicorn who will do anything to become queen of Enchanted Valley. She'll even steal the magical lockets if she has to. She won't give them back until the unicorns crown her queen.

Selena

Queen Aurora

Queen Aurora rules over Enchanted Valley and is in charge of friendship; there's nothing more important than her friends. She has a silver crown and a beautiful coat which can change colour.

The Crystal King looks after a neighbouring valley, and is a dear friend to Queen Aurora. He wears a crown of sparkling crystals on his head, and has a glittering silver mane and tail.

The Crystal

Spellford

Enchanted Valley

Enchanted Cottage

Golden Palace

An Enchanted Valley lies a twinkle away,
Where beautiful unicorns live, laugh and play.
You can visit the mermaids, or go for a ride,
So much fun to be had, but dangers can hide!

Your friends need your help – this is how you know:
A keyring lights up with a magical glow.
Whirled off like a dream, you won't want to leave.
Friendship forever, when you truly believe.

Story One

★★★★★★★★★★

A Giant Celebration

Chapter One
The Best Idea

Emily and Aisha stood in a meadow, surrounded by clouds of wildflowers. Petals flew through the air like confetti, sticking to their clothes and hair.

Aisha reached out to stroke the petals of a papery red poppy that bobbed beneath her hand. It was too beautiful

 13

to pick. Instead, she bent to pick a fluffy
dandelion clock and held it up to her
best friend.

"Make a wish and blow!" she cried.

Emily screwed her eyes tight. "I wish … I wish … I wish we were back in Enchanted Valley." She took a huge breath and blew, sending the seeds dancing away on the breeze.

Enchanted Valley was a special secret place that the girls had visited on many occasions. It almost felt like a second home to them now!

As if by magic, Emily's pocket began to glow.

Aisha felt a tingle run through her body.

The girls both knew it *was* magic!

Emily pulled out her crystal unicorn keyring. Aisha reached into her pocket and took out her identical glowing keyring. They grinned at one another.

"Your wish came true!" Aisha laughed.

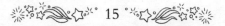

They touched the tips of the glowing horns together and sparkles appeared in the air all around them. They held hands as they felt their feet lift off the ground. There was the odd sensation of being carried through the air, light as swans' feathers.

They felt their feet land on soft grass and they knew even before the sparkles

cleared that this was the emerald carpet of Enchanted Valley.

The girls were standing at the bottom of a hill leading up to the most beautiful golden palace. Roses climbed all over the walls and the turrets were twisted, like unicorn horns. A golden drawbridge lowered over the sparkly blue moat and Queen Aurora came trotting out.

Her coat was all the colours of a
beautiful sunrise, shifting between yellows,
pinks and oranges, and her streaming
mane and tail were pure, rippled gold. A
tiny silver crown sat snugly behind her
golden horn, and around her neck was
one of the most magical things in the
whole of Enchanted Valley: the Friendship
locket. Every grown-up unicorn in
Enchanted Valley had their
own magical locket
that helped them take
care of something in
the valley. Queen
Aurora looked after
Friendship, because
that was one of the
most powerful and
important things of all.

"It's so good to see you!" she cried as the girls wrapped their arms around her neck.

"Did you hear me wishing to come back?" Emily asked.

Queen Aurora shook her head, and her mane rippled in the breeze. "No, dear, I'm afraid I didn't. I have been a little distracted ..."

"Is it Selena again?" Aisha asked.

Selena was a mean unicorn who wanted to steal Queen Aurora's crown and rule Enchanted Valley herself. The two friends had helped fight her off many times before.

"No," said Queen Aurora, looking a little sad. "It's just that the Crystal King is going home and I thought you would want to say goodbye."

As she spoke, another unicorn came clip-clopping over the drawbridge. His coat was gleaming white and his silver mane glittered as he dipped his nose to meet that of Queen Aurora. They shared a gentle glance, before turning to Aisha and Emily. The two royal unicorns had become such special friends.

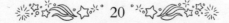

"It is time for me to leave," the king said. He gave a brave smile, but Aisha could see that his heart was full of regret. "You have all been so kind to me, but I must return to protect my own kingdom."

Aisha looked down at her hands sadly and saw she was still gripping the dandelion stalk. Beside her, Emily clasped a posy of flowers she had picked – daisies, primroses and buttercups. Before Emily knew what she was doing, she held them out to the Crystal King.

"These are for you," she said softly.

"Beautiful," the Crystal King sighed.

"Just like a bouquet you'd get at a wedding!" Aisha said.

There was a short pause, then Queen Aurora let out a whinny of delight and shook her golden mane.

"You've given me the best idea!" she
cried to the girls. She turned to the king,
a shy look on her face. "Dear King,
would you stay here and ... marry me?"

"Marry!" the king gasped.

"If you'd like to," the queen said, her
voice trembling.

Aisha and Emily reached to grip each
other's hands tight as they stared at

the king, hoping he'd say what they so wanted him to say.

The shocked king cleared his throat. "Well," he began, gazing at Queen Aurora. "I think that's … that's …" He gave a neigh of delight. "I think that's the best idea I ever heard! Yes! My answer is YES!"

Chapter Two
Bridal Bower

A royal wedding! The girls jumped up and down in delight. Who could imagine anything better in the whole wide world?

"We may have to be apart sometimes as we each rule our kingdoms," the king said, looking into Aurora's eyes.

"As long as I'm married to you, I don't

mind!" the queen replied.

"We'll make it work," the Crystal King added softly.

The girls sprang forward to hug them both. "Congratulations!" they cried.

The queen nuzzled her husband-to-be's nose, looking happier than the girls had ever seen her. Her eyes glowed as she raised her head and gave out the gentlest cry. "Heartsong!"

The girls looked around in confusion. There was no one else here. Who could Queen Aurora be talking to?

But moments later, the sound of hooves could be heard and a unicorn galloped through the air into view. Heartsong's golden tail flew out behind her as the peach colour of her glossy coat caught the sunshine. She came to land before them, three lockets jingling around her throat.

"Yes, Your Majesties?" she said, and bowed. The girls could see a very hopeful look on her face.

"Heartsong, we need your help to plan a wedding," said Aurora. The hair on her cheeks shifted to pink, as if she was blushing.

"That's the very best news!" Heartsong's words floated out on the air like a song. She turned to the girls. "And you must be Emily and Aisha. I've heard so much about you. I'm in charge of weddings in Enchanted Valley. Would you like to see my three lockets?"

"Yes, please!" the girls chorused. Some very special unicorns had three lockets, instead of just one. Heartsong bent her head so that they could admire the trinkets around her neck. "This one," said Heartsong, pointing her nose at a locket with a shower of confetti inside, "is for Celebrations. This one," and she pointed

to one with a branching tree inside, "is for Family. And can you guess what this one is?" She pointed to the third locket, which held a pair of linked rings.

Emily and Aisha shook their heads.

Heartsong's eyes twinkled as she glanced at Aurora and the Crystal King.

"This one is for True Love."

Both girls let out a sigh of happiness.

"Heartsong, we would like to be married today," said Queen Aurora.

"Today?" squeaked Emily.

"That's a lot to organise in one day," Aisha worried.

Heartsong laughed. "It's easy when we have magic! But there's no time to lose. Now, first things first. You will need to choose your bridesmaids."

Queen Aurora touched her velvety nose to the girls' hands. "I would like it to be you two!"

The girls gasped and beamed at one another. Emily had always dreamed of wearing a bridesmaid's dress! Aisha loved to imagine carrying a bride's soft, lacy veil between her hands.

"Yes please!" they chorused.

"Decision made!" Heartsong said. "Now, we have a lot to do. First stop, we need to go to Bridal Bower."

"That's where all the Enchanted Valley weddings are held," Aurora explained.

"Climb on my back," Heartsong invited the girls.

They did as she said, Aisha holding her mane gently, then all three unicorns launched into the sky!

The fields, woods and hills of Enchanted Valley spread out below them, like a beautiful green blanket. They weaved in and out of fluffy white clouds, waving at the birds they passed on the way. This was the best fun! Then, ahead, they saw a huge, flat cloud with a bright, perfect rainbow arched over it.

"Wow, look at that amazing rainbow!" Emily said, pointing.

"Welcome to Bridal Bower!" Heartsong said.

To the girls' surprise, she dipped her nose and landed right on the flat cloud. Aurora and the Crystal King landed beside her. The girls slid down from

Heartsong's back. The cloud was soft, but firm, like a mattress.

Aisha couldn't resist a cartwheel. "Amazing!" she cried as she landed in the downy white.

They heard a bark and turned to see a massive cloud shooting towards them.

"Fluffy!" called Emily.

The girls were thrilled to see their friend the cloud puppy again. They had had many adventures with him in the past.

"Hello, girls!" Fluffy called. "Is there a wedding going on?"

"Yes, it's ours," Aurora announced. "And Fluffy, you can be ring bearer!"

Fluffy wagged his tail so hard, he almost swept them all off the cloud! "I can't wait!"

Heartsong gathered everyone in. "Now, Your Majesties, I have some ideas. What about pink petal confetti and rainbow streamers?" As she spoke, pink petals rained down from above, and rainbow streamers exploded out of nowhere.

The king and queen nodded excitedly. "And I thought some lovebirds could sing a special new duet for the occasion," Heartsong suggested. A pair of multi-coloured birds swooped past, trilling a sweet little melody.

Queen Aurora's eyes sparkled with delight.

"What about a firework display?" Emily suggested.

"Ooh yes, for after the ceremony," Aisha agreed.

The king and queen shared a delighted smile.

"I'll send a message to the dragons," Heartsong said. "They create the best fireworks in the kingdom."

A sudden thought struck Aisha. "Once you are married, will you get a locket of your own?" she asked the Crystal King. The girls knew that the king had magic

of his own, but because he wasn't from
the valley, he didn't have a locket.

The king frowned in thought. "I don't
know!"

"Hmm. I don't either," Aurora said.
"The magic of the valley is beyond what
any of us can understand."

The Crystal King cuddled up to the
queen. "I don't need
a locket," he
murmured.
"Just a
lifetime
with you."
The
words were
hardly out
of his mouth,
when the cloud

they were standing on turned dark grey. With a *crash!* and a *flash!* a silver unicorn with a twilight-blue mane and tail appeared in the sky. Selena!

She began talking in a high, screechy voice. "*A lifetime with yooooou?!*" she

mocked, repeating the Crystal King's words. "Oh, please!" She shook herself all over, as though a hundred spiders were creeping over her glossy coat. "Who needs love? I don't have it, and I'm perfectly fine!"

Aisha felt her tummy twist and realised that she was feeling sorry for Selena, for

the first time ever.

Emily thought how awful it must be to have no one to love, or be loved by!

"I won't stay and watch this sickening scene," Selena said. "I just came to tell you that it's time to make me queen."

The Crystal King rolled his eyes. "Why would we do that?"

A strange booming sound could be heard, coming from beyond a hill. It got louder all the time. *Boom. Boom. BOOM!*

Selena's eyes narrowed in wicked pleasure. "Why don't you ask my friend?"

Chapter Three
A Royal Kidnap

Emily's heart thudded in time to the booming sound and Aisha's mouth turned suddenly dry. Fluffy yelped and dived for cover.

A figure appeared over the horizon – bigger than anything they'd ever seen before. A head as big as a house,

shoulders as broad as a barn, a huge
leather belt around a giant tummy and
legs that were taller than a skyscraper.
It was a giant! He towered over Bridal
Bower and snarled. The rush of his

breath whipped the girls' hair back.

Selena went to fly around the giant's head. "Perfect timing," she said. "I was just saying that it's time for me to take my place on the throne."

The giant grunted in agreement.

Aisha had never felt so frightened, and she could see that Emily's face had turned very pale, too. But they wouldn't run away and hide. They'd stand by their friends.

"You know what to do!" Selena said.

The giant reached out one enormous hand and swiped at the friends on the cloud.

"DUCK!" yelled Aisha.

She and Emily threw themselves down on to the white fluff.

When they looked back up, to their relief, the three unicorns were still standing.

But then Heartsong let out a wail. "No! My lockets!"

There, hooked around the giant's littlest

finger, were the three glimmering lockets.

"Yes!" Selena said, laughing.

"Give those back now!" cried Queen Aurora.

The girls ran to stand at her side.

"He'll do nothing of the sort," smirked Selena, her purple eyes flashing.

"They don't belong to you, Selena." The Crystal King's voice was deeper and more booming than the girls had ever heard before. "Give those lockets back."

"Oh, make him be quiet," Selena ordered the giant.

Before anyone had time to duck again, the giant swiped with his other hand and grabbed the Crystal King! All they could see of him was his tail, swishing out from inside the giant's meaty fist.

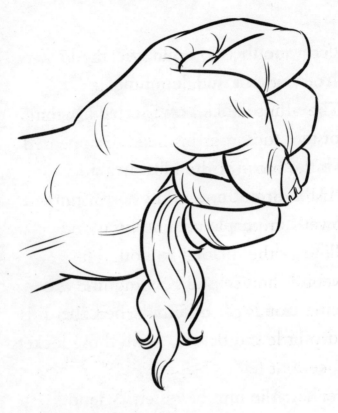

"No!" Aurora cried.

"Put him down!" Emily yelled.

Selena's eyes flashed. "If you want your precious king and lockets back, you know what to do – make me queen!"

Aisha stamped her foot. "Never!"

"Say goodbye to your love, then," Selena cackled, swooping away.

The giant walked off too, his booming footsteps fading as his head disappeared over the brow of the hill.

Aisha looked around to see Bridal Bower's streamers turning grey and falling to the ground like ash. The lovebirds had stopped cooing and the gentle clouds of confetti turned into sharp little shards of ice that fell over them in a hailstorm.

A tear trickled down Queen Aurora's nose. "Selena's taken my love!" she cried.

"Whatever will we do?"

Emily placed her fists on her hips. "Well, not give up, that's for sure!" she said.

"Definitely not!" Aisha added. "We'll get the king back, and the lockets too!"

Queen Aurora smiled at the girls. "Thank you both. You're right – we can do it if we stay strong."

"Always!" the girls cried.

"We must follow that giant!" Aisha suggested. "At least he'll be easy to find."

"Indeed. After him!" the queen cried, in a royal command.

Emily climbed on to her back and, as Aisha began to follow, Heartsong stepped forward.

"I'm coming to help too! Aisha, you climb on my back."

Aisha did as she said.

"Me too!" Fluffy yapped. "That giant is scary but together, we can stop him and Selena!"

Aurora quickly summoned a bluebird messenger to ask Ember the phoenix to guard the palace while they were gone. Then they soared into the air, chasing after the giant and the poor king he had kidnapped.

Chapter Four
Firework Friends

Aurora, Heartsong and Fluffy climbed higher to fly over the top of the hill. They saw another sloping peak ahead of them – but this one had a column of smoke and sparks drifting out of the top.

"It's Firework Mountain," Heartsong said in a rush. "Why is he going there?"

"Maybe the dragons could help us!"
Aisha cried, remembering all their other
adventures with the fiery creatures who
lived on Firework Mountain.

As they drew close to the mountain,
they spotted glittering figures lounging
in one of the hot pools that dotted the
mountain slopes.

"There!" Emily pointed. "There
are the dragons!"

Aisha peered
down.

She could see three big dragons enjoying their steamy bath. There was one with golden scales, one with silver and one with bronze. "Hello, Sparky. Hi, Smoky. Hey, Coal!" she called down. The girls were old friends with the dragons. They had been some of the first creatures Emily and Aisha had ever met in Enchanted Valley! "We need your help!"

The friends glided in to land next to the pool. The air was steamy and hot.

All three dragons looked very worried as the girls explained what had happened and pointed at the huge giant heading towards their mountain.

"Can you help us?" Aisha asked.

"Maybe you could use your fireworks to distract him so we can get the king and the lockets back," said Emily.

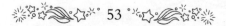

"Good idea!" cried Coal, little flames shooting from his mouth.

"We won't let that naughty giant get away with this," Sparky declared, climbing out of the hot pool and shaking his golden scales.

"Let's go," said Smoky, launching himself straight out of the pool and up into the air.

The three dragons soared into the sky, their brilliant scales glittering in the sunlight. They all swooped down to the volcano crater and then reappeared with armfuls of colourful little packages: the magic fireworks!

Aurora, Heartsong and Fluffy followed them back up into the air, carrying the girls on their backs.

"Rocket – launch!" Sparky blew into the air, and purple sparkles shot from his mouth.

The girls held their breath as the giant's eye was caught by the beautiful sight. He seemed intrigued …

But then the sparkles fizzled out into nothing.

Sparky looked confused.

"Maybe it got wet?" suggested Coal. "Hey giant, watch this!" He blew a spout of fire which burned brightly – and then stuttered and stopped, leaving just some twisted grey debris to fall to the ground.

The giant had turned away from the dragons – clearly bored – and carried on towards the mountain.

"I don't know what's wrong!" Smoky cried. He twisted in somersaults in the air.

"Catherine wheel – spin!"

But the Catherine wheel flopped from his mouth and dropped straight to the ground.

Aisha had an idea of why this was happening. "It's because of Heartsong's Celebrations locket!"

"Of course!" Heartsong agreed. "Fireworks are for celebrations, so they're not going to work without the locket."

The girls felt their hearts sink. How could they distract the giant now?

The giant let out a booming laugh, as his fists tightened around the lockets and the Crystal King. The king let out a small whinny of pain.

"You shan't fool me!" the giant said. He reached a hand high above his head – which was very high indeed. The three lockets dangled on their chains as the giant reached out above the smoking crater of the volcano.

"I'm going to drop the lockets here!" he said. "Just like Selena told me to. Goodbye to celebrations, family and true love! Queen Aurora will never have her wedding now. Enchanted Valley won't have a king, after all!"

Chapter Five
Air Dance

The girls stared at one another. They needed another plan – and fast!

"Quick, Fluffy! Can you cover the volcano with clouds?" said Aisha.

"Right away." Fluffy beamed. He soared towards the mountain. From his paws, a set of clouds appeared, like white

meringues that covered the top of the volcano.

"But clouds won't stop the giant from dropping anything in," said Emily, in a low voice. "The lockets will just fall straight through."

"So we'll have to catch them as they fall," said Aisha. "And the clouds will stop the giant from seeing us!"

They flew behind Fluffy – Emily on Aurora's back, and Aisha on Heartsong's.

The giant was still slowly reaching his hand over the crater. They could see the Celebrations locket dangling from the tip of his finger. "One," he boomed, letting the locket slip off.

It fell down, disappearing through Fluffy's white clouds.

"Quick!" Aisha urged.

Aurora and Heartsong dived through the clouds and into the crater. It was gloomy, and the girls blinked in the darkness.

A moment later, Aurora and Heartsong's horns began to glow with golden light, like two torches. "There it is!" Aisha cried as she spotted the twinkling locket tumbling down into the darkness, falling like confetti. Heartsong sped towards it. Aisha reached out to grab it, but her hands missed, closing over thin air. She felt her stomach jolt as the locket dropped further into the crater.

"Emily!" she cried. "Yours!"

Emily lunged forward as the locket

whizzed past her nose. Her fingers closed and …

"Yes!" she cried, feeling the warm gold of the locket grasped in her hands. She reached up and shook her hand in the air. "I have it!"

The two unicorns
soared back up
and burst through
the clouds.
Emily held the
locket in the air
triumphantly.

The giant was
still standing over the
crater, a second locket dangling from
his fingertips. When he saw the locket
in Emily's hand, a scowl spread over
his enormous face. "Not fair!" His eyes
narrowed crossly. "Well, you won't get the
others!" He turned and bounded away
with huge, earth-shaking steps.

Aurora and Heartsong landed on the
rocks at the edge of the volcano. Emily
scrambled down from Aurora's back. She

walked over to Heartsong and held out her hand to reveal the precious locket on the flat of her palm.

"Yours, I believe," she said.

Heartstong's eyes brimmed with delight. "It is indeed," she said, dipping her head so that Emily could place the locket back where it belonged.

Instantly, Firework Mountain exploded from behind them, with beautiful sparks of red and gold. The dragons cheered and set off some fireworks of their own. Aisha and Emily let out whoops of delight and gasps of wonder as fireworks sang and fizzed in the air, filling it with all the colours of the rainbow.

Heartsong's horn glowed for a moment and then a cloud of confetti was raining over them all, in the softest petals of pink,

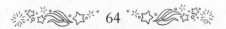

turquoise and buttercup yellow. "Thank you for saving my Celebrations locket," she said. Aisha and Emily smiled at each other, but there was sadness in their eyes. Their mission was very far from over! They walked over to stand by Aurora, who was shivering despite the volcano's warmth.

The queen's noble gaze shifted from the friends towards the distant horizon, where the giant had disappeared. She swallowed hard, tears gathering beneath her long eyelashes. "We still need to find the Crystal King, and the other lockets."

Aisha and Emily looked at each other, determined. "And we will," they promised.

Then off they flew …

Story Two

⋆·∗·★·★·★·★·★·∗·⋆

A Family Fail

Chapter One
A Flurry of Feathers

"There's no time to lose – we must follow the giant," Emily said. A trail of huge footsteps cut across the valley and over the hill.

"You lot go on. I'll need to stay here," Fluffy said, "and clear up my clouds."

"What a good dog you are," Aisha said,

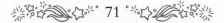

and Fluffy wagged his tail.

They climbed on to their unicorn friends' backs, waved goodbye to Fluffy and the dragons, and the four of them took to the air. They followed the footprints towards the crest of the hill. The giant's stride was so huge that it was

difficult to keep track from one footprint
to the next – and when they arrived at
the top of the hill, the giant was a tiny
dot disappearing over the horizon.

Aurora and Heartsong were panting
from flying so fast – and they still hadn't
caught up!

"This is no good," Emily said, her hands tangled in Heartsong's gold mane. "We'll never catch him up. He's so big that even one step is an enormous distance! If only he were smaller ..."

"That's it!" Aisha snapped her fingers. "What if we could shrink him down? Maybe Hob will have a shrinking potion." Their goblin friend, Hob, was the best potion-maker in the valley. He had helped them so many times before on their adventures.

They steered round and headed over towards Hob's cave. Their route took them past Ember the phoenix's nest, high in the clouds. There was the most terrible squabbling noise. All six of Ember's chicks were pecking at each other and sending out tiny sparks of fire. Their little bodies tumbled over one another as they fought for the best spot in the nest, and angry squawks carried up on the air.

"Get off me!"

"That's my place!"

"Wait till I tell on you!"

"Oh dear, and Ember is away guarding the palace!" Aisha gasped.

"What is wrong with them?" Emily wondered. "They're usually so loving to one another."

"I think it's my missing Family locket," said Heartsong, sadly. "Now that it's gone, families can't live in harmony."

Aisha didn't want to think about that at all! She hated it when her parents argued.

"We'd better get that locket back," she said, a flurry of urgency rising inside her.

"Just as soon as we've saved the Crystal King," Emily reminded her.

Queen Aurora gave a sigh of longing, just at the sound of his name.

"Come on," Aisha said as Aurora started to descend towards a familiar cave. "Let's see what potions Hob has!"

Chapter Two
Smallifying Seaweed

The unicorns came down to land in a flurry of glistening hooves. Aisha and Emily slid from their backs and they stuck their heads into the gloomy entrance of the cave.

"Hob?" they called. "Are you there?"

"Girls, is that you?" a faint voice called

back. "Come on down!"

The girls, Aurora and Heartsong all filed into the narrow tunnel that led down to Hob's crammed cavern. Crystals in the ceiling were lit by glimmering lanterns. The walls were lined with shelves, stuffed with every potion ingredient under the sun.

In the centre of the cavern was a wooden workbench. A small figure in a long purple gown and a pointy hat was mixing something in a bowl with a big, long-handled spoon.

"Hob!" the girls cried.

"Girls!" he exclaimed. "It's lovely to see you again!" He carefully put down his spoon and gave them each a hug. He was only half their height, and the tip of his hat tickled their chins.

Hob blinked through his big golden spectacles as he saw Queen Aurora and Heartsong as well. "Your Majesty; Heartsong! What can I do for you today?" He bowed low.

"Hob, we need you to make us a potion!" Aisha said.

"A shrinking potion!" Emily added.

"The Crystal King is in terrible danger and we think it will help us rescue him!"

Hob shook his head, mournfully. "I have lots of potions that can make you grow, but I'm all out of shrinking potion." He went to a shelf and indicated an empty glass jar with a label on the front. The girls went over and read the curly writing on the label. It said:

Smallifying Seaweed

"Looks like I'm out of the ingredients to make more, too. I usually get it from the mermaids' lagoon," Hob explained. He nodded at the star-speckled liquid on his bench. "But I've been so busy making extra sparkle for the Glitter Flitters ..." His words drifted off – he looked ready

to burst into tears at the thought of
letting down Queen Aurora!

"Don't worry," Emily said, placing a
hand on his. "We'll go to the lagoon and
get some more for you."

"Thank you!" he cried. "And I will get
the rest of the ingredients ready."

"Yes," Aisha said firmly. "We'll meet
you back here."

"Right!" Hob cried. "Smallifying
Seaweed is a bright lime green, and
wiggly, like a worm."

A moment later, the four of them
were flying through the air towards
the mermaid lagoon. The girls had
been there many times before. It was a
beautiful, warm pool, separated from the
sea by a line of gleaming rocks.

But when they arrived, the girls gasped

and the queen cried out in horror.

There wasn't any water in the lagoon!

Everywhere they looked, they saw
moss and stones, sand and mud – but no
water at all. In the heart of the lagoon,
the mermaids lay across rocks. They were
stranded! Their tails flapped weakly and
their long, usually sleek hair had turned
dry and frizzly, sticking out like straw.

"Help!" they cried. "Our water's all dried up!"

The mermaids held out their arms, but there was no way they could reach the friends.

"How did this happen?" Aisha wondered.

Queen Aurora pointed her horn towards a large, oval shape in the mud.

"Look," she said.

It was another giant footprint!

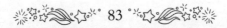

Chapter Three
Flying Mermaids!

"Has a giant been here?" Emily called over to the mermaids.

"Yes! How did you guess?" Pearl called back.

Emily pointed at the footprint in the mud.

Pearl nodded miserably. "He came and

drank all of our water! And even after that he said he was *still* thirsty!" She threw her cousin a filthy look. "It was Neptune's fault. If he hadn't been singing so loudly, the giant would never have spotted us."

Neptune folded his arms across his tummy. "*My* fault?" he exploded. "You asked me to sing for you. Begged me to!"

Pearl pulled a face. "Why would I do that?" she asked. "You have a voice like a screech owl."

Everyone gasped – how rude!

"Oh dear,"

Heartsong said, "my missing locket is making families argue all over the kingdom."

Aisha piped up before Neptune could continue. "We need to get you out of here."

Aisha was still sitting on Heartsong's back. Now, Heartsong flew up into the air and landed delicately on the rock where Pearl was sitting.

"Now what?" Aisha wondered aloud. Mermaids couldn't just climb on to unicorns' backs like she and Emily did, because they had no legs!

Aurora flew over, with Emily on her back, landing on the rock where Neptune was stranded.

Emily leaned down and held out both hands to Neptune. "Hold on!" she said.

Neptune reached up and gripped her hands tightly.

Aurora took off again, lifting Neptune up into the air so that his tail dangled down.

Emily found he was surprisingly light. It was like holding up a big marshmallow!

Below, Neptune giggled. "Wow, flying is

great! Almost as good as swimming!"

Meanwhile, back on the rocks, Aisha copied what Emily had done, reaching down to Pearl. Heartsong lifted them both up into the air.

"Faster! Faster!" Pearl joked.

It was only a short flight over to the sea. The unicorns landed knee-deep in the water and the girls let go of the mermaids' hands. Pearl and Neptune slid away into the sea.

The girls and the unicorns quickly made several trips back and forth, until all the mermaids were back in the water. They had to save the Crystal King and get the lockets back, but they couldn't leave the mermaids stuck like this.

"Thank you!" the mermaids called. Their hair flowed softly and their scales

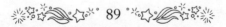

glowed beautifully once more.

"We almost forgot!" Aisha said. "May we take some Smallifying Seaweed from the lagoon? It might help us defeat the giant."

"Of course!" Pearl cried. "There is some around the base of the rock I was sitting on. Take as much as you need. Good luck!"

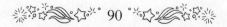

Then she turned and dived down under the waves.

Queen Aurora and Heartsong carried the girls back to the dry lagoon. Emily and Aisha slid off the unicorns' backs into thick, squishy mud. There, on Pearl's rock, was some lime-green seaweed.

"It really *does* look like wiggly worms," said Emily.

She gathered some up, shoving the seaweed into her pockets. Aisha did the same. She could tell that all the others were thinking the same thing as she was: *This just has to work!*

Chapter Four
Truth Time

Aurora and Heartsong flew so quickly that it didn't take long at all to arrive at Hob's cave!

The girls ran inside, their pockets bulging, with Aurora and Heartsong hot on their heels. Hob was already at his bench, mixing so hard that his spoon was

a blur, smatters of yellow liquid all over his apron.

"Tip it in!" he told them.

Aisha and Emily stuffed their hands into their pockets, pulling out the Smallifying Seaweed. It looked so sad and crumpled, but they crushed it into the potion, being sure to scatter it across the bowl.

Hob picked up his spoon again and began stirring.

"If this works properly it'll make emerald smoke," Hob explained. "Cross your fingers!" The girls did as they were told and held their hands up, all fingers crossed. Heartsong and Aurora even crossed their hooves!

They waited and waited as Hob stirred, until … yes! A curl of emerald smoke

drifted up out of the bowl.

"It's working!" Hob cried, stirring even
harder. Suddenly he stopped and plunged
the mixing bowl of now-green liquid
into a huge bowl of ice. "Now we need
to cool it down." When it was ready he
reached for a couple of tiny bottles made
of amber glass. They
glowed orange in
the candlelight
as he poured
the cooled
shrinking
potion in and
then added a
cork stopper to
each bottle. He
handed them over
to Aisha and Emily.

"Take care of them," Hob warned. "Any leaks, and you might end up as small as ladybirds! All you need is a tiny drop," he explained, wiping his hands on his leather apron. "Just. One. Drop. Understand?"

The friends nodded and ran back outside, calling "Thank you!" over their shoulders.

"Now, how do we find the giant?" Heartsong asked, looking anxiously at the queen. All three of them were so glad that the royal unicorn had come with them on this quest. She knew more about Enchanted Valley than anyone else.

Aurora's brow creased in a frown as she thought hard. "The mermaids told us the giant drank their whole lagoon but he was still thirsty," she said, her words slowly emerging as an idea formed. Her face lit up. "We should go to the Whistling Waterfall! There is so much clean, pure water there!"

"Good thinking," Emily said.

Soon, the friends were all in the sky again. They were desperate to save the Crystal King.

They came down to land beside the tinkling sound of the waterfall. It was like listening to an orchestra full of triangles and violins, making the most gorgeous music. Emily felt as though she was back at a school concert, even though she could see all around her the drifting ferns and pillows of moss that grew beside a waterfall. A soft spray of water tickled their faces and they looked up to the very top of the Whistling Waterfall, searching for signs of the giant.

But then the sound of angry voices floated through the air.

"Get off!"

"That's mine!"

Two familiar little fluffy figures were standing amongst the ferns, looking very cross with one another! It was Walt and Wendy Woffly, the guinea hogs.

Emily and Aisha had met the Woffly family on a previous adventure in the valley, and they had become good friends with the twins.

Walt's ginger fur stood on end as he glared at his sister.

Wendy wrinkled her little piggy snout at him. "The pebble is *mine*. I saw it!"

The girls noticed she was clutching a small pebble all the colours of the rainbow in her honey-coloured paw.

"But *I* want it!" Walt retorted. "You already have lots of nice pebbles!"

"So do you!" Wendy snapped.

Emily felt her heart sinking. "Oh dear, Walt and Wendy are usually so kind to one another," she whispered to the others.

"It's because of my Family locket," Heartsong murmured back, looking distressed. "Oh, how I wish I could help!"

Aisha was about to go and stand between the furious siblings, when Aurora pointed beyond the waterfall with her horn. "Over there," she whispered.

The friends looked to where she was pointing, and there was the giant. He was so big that he had looked like part of the hill as he knelt at the edge of the waterfall, plants crushed beneath his huge knees. Didn't he know to look after nature?

His hands – big as spades! – reached into the waterfall, bringing crystal-clear water up to his open mouth, where his yellow teeth gave off an awful glow.

Slurp!

He was making the most terrible noises, not drinking politely at all! There was no

sign of the Crystal King anywhere. But on a rock by the giant's side, there was something else beautiful – Heartsong's Family locket!

"Let's grab that locket," Emily decided quickly. "We might not get another chance! And then we can find the king."

The four friends all nodded in

agreement. Emily and Aisha were careful to stay quiet: they moved … very … slowly … and … silently.

One by one, they tiptoed around the edge of the pool at the bottom of the waterfall. It was tricky for the unicorns to tiptoe with their hooves, but they did their best, avoiding stones.

Closer and closer they crept, as the giant plunged his clumsy hands into the water yet again. He sent out a spray that covered them all in ice-cold water, but the friends managed to shiver without crying out. Just a little closer …

Suddenly, a huge hand snatched out!

The giant scooped up the locket in his

fist and leapt to his feet, sending a tremor through the ground.

"Oi!" he cried, even though they'd all been trying to move ever so slowly. His eyes glinted with jubilation. "I know what you're up to!" He clutched the locket to his chest. "It's mine."

Emily pulled back her shoulders. "Actually, I think you'll find it belongs to Heartsong."

The peach-coloured unicorn gave a snort of agreement. "Give it back."

But the giant wasn't listening. He tucked the locket in his pocket, reached out his two massive hands – and scooped up Aisha and Emily! Now they were captured too!

Chapter Five
A Glimmer of Hope

The girls screamed as they felt their legs dangling between the giant's fingers.

"What do you think you're doing?" he shouted, his words as loud as a thunderclap. The girls wished they could cover their ears. Emily could feel her whole body trembling in his grasp.

Aisha dared to look up into his face. It was like looking at a craggy mountain.

"Tell me now, or I'll crush you!" he boomed.

There was nothing for it but to tell the truth.

"We wanted to make you shrink," Emily admitted bravely. "If you'll let us reach into our pockets, we can show you."

The giant stared at her for a moment, then he turned his hands around and opened his fingers so that the girls were lying in his open palms. Carefully, they each sat up and pulled out the amber glass bottles from their pockets, showing the giant the labels that read: *Shrinking Potion*.

"We couldn't keep up with you and we need to rescue our friend, the king!" Aisha explained.

"We don't know what Selena will do to him," said Emily.

The giant gently lowered them to the ground, his glare fading. Then he plopped

himself down on a nearby rock and it only cracked in three places.

"A shrinking potion?" A thoughtful look crossed his face. "I've always wanted to be smaller, you know …"

"Really?" the girls asked together. They saw a glimmer of hope. Was there a way to bring the giant on to their side? From behind the giant's back, Aurora and Heartsong gave their friends an encouraging nod. *Keep going!*

Emily took a big gulp. "Would you like us to help?"

An enormous tear, the size of a beach ball, rolled down the giant's nose. The girls had to dodge out of the way as it crashed to the ground, spraying them all with salt water. "More than anything!" He gulped back a sob. "Selena promised

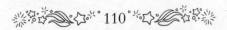

she would use her magic to make me
normal. That's – that's why I'm helping
her. I'm sick of being so tall!"

The girls felt their hearts swell with
sympathy for the poor, sad giant.

Aisha stepped forward and put a hand
on the end of his boot. "But there isn't
any such thing as normal, really."

Emily nodded in agreement. "We're all made to be different," she said kindly.

The giant nodded. "I know, I know. I just …" He looked at them with hope in his huge eyes. "Could I be … less different?"

"Of course!" Who were the girls to deny a giant his hope of happiness?

Aisha held out her bottle. "Now, read the instructions very carefully."

The instructions read:

To be taken once a day.
Small sips only!

But the giant didn't stop to read it. He grabbed it from her hand, tore the cork from the bottle's neck and swallowed the whole thing in one!

"No!" the girls cried together, as the unicorns whinnied with distress.

Too late!

Before their eyes, the giant shivered and shimmered and shrank down, down, down until …

Emily crouched down and held out her hand. "Need a lift?" she asked with a chuckle.

The giant clambered up into her palm, laughing. "Oops, maybe I drank a bit much!" he giggled. "But this is better."

Aisha reached for the locket, which had fallen into a pillow of moss. Now that the giant was so small, it was too big for him to hold.

Heartsong trotted over and Aisha slipped the Family locket over her head, to sit next to the Celebrations locket.

Immediately, Walt and Wendy stopped squabbling.

Walt padded over to his sister and threw his arms around her neck. "I'm so sorry, Wendy. You keep the pebble. I want you to have it."

Wendy beamed as she gave her brother a big cuddle. "Why don't we share it?" she suggested.

Aurora's eyes squeezed tight with longing. "Families …" she said, almost to herself. "I wish I could have one of my own."

"You will!" Aisha cried.

"But not without the Crystal King," Emily added. "He's the first part of your family."

"Well, then," Heartsong decided, "we need to find him!"

All four of them turned to gaze at the tiny figure in the centre of Emily's palm.

"Can you help us?" Aisha asked.

"Of course," the now tiny giant said, smiling at them all. "Selena has taken him to her castle. Heartsong's True Love

locket is there, too!"

At last, they knew how to find the Crystal King and get the last locket back!

Story Three

★·˙*˙·★·★·˙*·★·˙*·★·˙*·★·˙

True Love Conquers All

Chapter One
Confetti Clouds

Aisha and Emily shivered as they caught sight of the jagged turrets and dark banners of Selena's castle. Even the wind seemed angry here, whipping the unicorns' manes up.

Emily felt the giant's body trembling between her hands.

"Gosh, it all looks so big, now that I'm small," he said, his teeth chattering. "Look at that horrible massive castle! And that huge moat! It's as wide as the sea!"

"Don't worry," said Emily. "Just because it's bigger than you, it doesn't mean it has to be scary." Even though she was trying to sound calm, she was scared herself. Selena's castle wasn't a nice place!

"What shall we call you now that you're not ... er ... giant?" Emily added.

"My name is Geoffrey," he said.

"An excellent name!" Aisha said, making him beam. Emily grinned too. Her friend was so good at boosting people up when they needed it most!

But as they slipped off the unicorns' backs, figures appeared around the moat which made them worry again. Dumpy figures, dressed in murky grey. Trolls!

The friends all ducked behind a big rock so that the trolls wouldn't see them.

"They're so much bigger than I remember!" Geoffrey squealed.

Aisha peeked out from behind the rock. "They're bigger than I remember, too," she muttered.

The others peered out and saw she was

right. These trolls were much taller and burlier than the ones Selena usually had guarding her castle!

"Oh dear." Aurora was weaving back and forth in anxiety behind the rock. "I don't … I don't …" She gave the girls an apologetic shake of her mane. "I don't think this is a good idea. I think we should go back to my castle."

"But … the Crystal King! Your wedding!" the girls reminded her.

"I don't know if I WANT there to be a wedding," the queen cried.

Aisha and Emily gasped.

"I know what's happening," Heartsong whispered. "It's my missing locket. Queen Aurora is doubting true love."

"Of course, you don't have to marry the Crystal King if you don't want to,"

Emily said gently, stroking Aurora's neck.

"No, everyone will understand – including him," Aisha reassured the queen. "But don't you think we ought to save him from Selena anyway?"

Queen Aurora lifted her head. "Of course. You are right, girls. Thank you."

The girls gave her a hug, then quickly squeezed one another's hands. They were pretty sure that Aurora would remember how much she loved the Crystal King as soon as they got the True Love locket back!

"Now, we just need a plan to get inside," said Heartsong, peeking out at the castle. "I can't see a way past those trolls. They're bound to spot us!"

Emily thought hard. "Actually, I bet there's one of us they won't see." She

carefully placed Geoffrey on the ground.
"Geoffrey, do you think you could sneak
past the trolls to lower the drawbridge?"

Geoffrey looked terrified. "But what if
they catch me?" he squeaked.

"Emily's right, they won't even see
you!" Aisha chimed in. "Did you notice
every little bug or mouse on the ground
when you were a giant?"

Geoffrey furrowed his brow as he
thought. "Well, no …"

"Because you were big, so you didn't
notice little things. Now, the trolls are big
and you are one of those little things,"
Aisha continued, and Emily thought
again about how good her friend was at
boosting people's confidence.

Without hesitating, Geoffrey ran
down the bank and swam past the trolls,

emerging beside the drawbridge. He rolled beneath the door and then the friends waited. With a creak … and a groan … and another creak … the drawbridge began to lower. They could see Geoffrey on the other side! Despite being small, he was still very strong and was turning the handle to lower the bridge.

The trolls were all gazing at the bridge, scratching their heads.

"How?" one grunted.

"Trouble?" another wondered.

"We can't cross the bridge while they're staring at it. We need to distract them," Aisha whispered.

"Leave it to me!" Heartsong said. She lifted her horn towards the sky. There was a sudden explosion of colour, and confetti began to dance through the air. It was all the colours of the rainbow.

"Urgh!" cried a troll.

"Disgusting!" said his friend.

The trolls all tried to shake the beautiful confetti off, as if it was freezing cold rain, then ran away to shelter beneath a tree.

With no one to guard the drawbridge, the way was clear.

Geoffrey waved a little hand. "Come on!"

The friends didn't need telling twice. They darted across the bridge, above the dirty, muddy water in the moat, and into the dark gloom of Selena's castle.

The girls knelt down and each held up a fingertip for Geoffrey to high five.

"We made it!" they exclaimed.

Chapter Two
Unlocking the Locket

The friends began to tiptoe through the creepy castle. It was dark and draughty, the exact opposite of Queen Aurora's beautiful and light golden palace.

Something small skittered over the floor past Emily's foot and she had to gulp back a gasp.

"Don't worry, it was probably just a little mouse," Geoffrey whispered cheerily from her shoulder.

Aisha took Emily's hand and gave it a squeeze. "We can do this," she whispered in Emily's other ear.

Just then, they heard a familiar wicked
cackle ringing through the halls. They
quickly followed the sound to Selena's
huge throne room. They all gathered
around a crack in the door and peered in.

"Oh, we're being ever so brave!"

Geoffrey murmured. The girls agreed with him.

The throne room was huge. The ceiling rose high above their heads, misted with smoke. There were portraits all along the walls – Emily guessed they were of other mean unicorns. They all looked a bit like Selena – nasty and sneering. She wondered if Selena had once had family to love her. But the portraits were so old and dusty, she guessed that there hadn't been any for a very long time. Yet again, she felt sorry for the evil unicorn. Did Selena really not believe in love?

Selena twitched with irritation on her throne. It was made of some sort of metal, the strands twisting around each other like thorny vines. "Well, this isn't right," she grumbled. "Not right at all! I feel disgusting. Almost … friendly. Ooey and gooey and – eurgh!" She shuddered.

"It's because she's wearing the True Love locket," Emily realised.

Sure enough, Heartsong's locket was nestled around Selena's neck.

"It *isn't* disgusting!" Heartsong whispered, indignantly. "It's the most wonderful feeling in the world!"

"I wonder if she'll realise that?" Aisha mused, quietly.

But suddenly, Selena dipped her head and ripped the locket off. "It's this that's making me soppy!"

Selena ran over to a safe in the corner of the throne room and hurled the locket inside. She slammed the door shut and turned a silver key. "That's *much* better," she crowed. "No room for love in this

castle!" She hung the key around her neck and trotted out of a side door.

The friends waited until the sound of Selena's hoofbeats had faded before they slipped inside the throne room.

"We must get that locket out," Queen Aurora said, walking over to the safe.

"But how can we without the key?" Heartsong asked.

"I've read about picking locks with hair grips," Emily said. "But I've never done it before."

"And we don't have any hair grips," Aisha added.

Emily realised everyone else was staring at her blankly. "If you don't have a key for a lock, sometimes you can slip something else inside and jiggle it around and unlock it that way ... Never mind, I

don't know how to do it anyway …" Her voice trailed off.

"What about if *we* could slip inside?" Aisha said. She pulled out the leftover bottle of Shrinking Potion. "I bet with just a couple of drops, we could stroll right through the keyhole!"

"Let's do it." Emily nodded, and moved Geoffrey to a safe place. "Hob has the potion to make us big again later."

"That's an amazing

plan!" Heartsong said.

"You girls always know what to do," Aurora added gratefully.

"You are very clever," said Geoffrey, gazing up at them.

With a *pop* Aisha released the cork and held the bottle to her mouth. It was the sweetest-tasting potion – a bit like candyfloss with a touch of caramel. She took a sip, then passed it to Emily.

They swallowed.

Right away, they felt all tingly and warm. Then, suddenly, the world exploded upwards, growing bigger and bigger! Except, Emily

realised with a jolt, it was actually them growing smaller and smaller.

Then the shrinking stopped and the girls were left standing next to a gleaming gold cliff, which they realised was actually Aurora's hoof!

Emily's voice came out in a squeak. "Ready?"

Aisha gave a tiny nod of her tiny head. "Ready!"

Heartsong let them climb on to her nose and lifted them up to the safe.

There was the keyhole,

leading into the dark safe beyond. Aisha
shuddered. She hoped Selena wasn't
keeping anything scary in there!

"Ready?" Emily whispered, sounding
nervous too.

Together, they
walked right
through the
keyhole. The
inside of the
lock was
made up of
a set of ridges,
with cogs
and wheels
and metal
parts that
fit snugly
together. It

was like a shiny tunnel. And on the other side, inside the safe, sat the glimmering locket of True Love.

"Yes!" said Emily. "We've got it!" she shouted back to the others.

But Aisha was frowning. The locket was too big to fit through the keyhole. "How do we get it out?"

Emily frowned too and walked back into the keyhole. She looked up at the cogs and wheels. "All we have to do is figure out how to move these cogs, get them into the right place, and the door will open," she said. "I think."

Emily wished she had time to sit down and draw a diagram so she could figure it all out properly but she knew they had to hurry.

She pushed the edge of one cog. Aisha

ran to help her push. Slowly, it turned with a *click*.

"Well done!" Aisha pushed the next one until that clicked too.

They moved along the row. Some cogs needed to turn further than others before they clicked into place.

Aisha pushed the final cog into position.

"Try it now!" Aisha called to her friends outside.

The girls crossed their fingers for luck as Aurora tried the handle. With a *click* and a *creak*, the door swung open.

They'd opened the safe from the inside!

"We did it!" they cried.

"Well done, girls!" Queen Aurora cheered quietly.

The two of them clambered back out and held the locket out to Heartsong. She dipped her head and they slipped the chain back over her neck. "Thank you, both," she said. "You have made sure the weddings of Enchanted Valley are safe. Now, it's time to find the groom." She turned to Queen Aurora. "That is, if he is still your groom?"

Queen Aurora's eyes were shining with tears. "Of course he is! My one true love. I can't wait to marry him."

The girls held tiny hands and squeezed. They had been sure that Aurora still loved the Crystal King.

A frown passed over Aurora's face. "But how will we find him?"

Heartsong gently touched her nose to the queen's. The True Love locket on her chest glowed. "Just follow your heart."

Chapter Three
Follow Your Heart

Queen Aurora stood as still as a statue for a moment, as if she was listening for music that nobody else could hear. Then she gasped. "I know where he is! Quick, girls!"

She bent her head so that the girls and Geoffrey could climb up her forehead

and sit nestled in her silver crown, on top of her soft golden mane. Then she led the way out into the courtyard, after pausing to check for trolls. Her horn pointed towards a doorway to the side of the courtyard. "Down there!"

Aurora pushed open the door with a hoof, the hinges creaking. A set of steps appeared, damp and slippery. Candles were set into the walls, lighting the way – and from far below they could hear a desperate whinny.

It was a voice that all of them recognised.

"My Crystal King!" Queen Aurora gasped.

She and Heartsong stepped into the gloom. The girls and Geoffrey held on tight to the rim of Aurora's crown as she

tipped forward and started to make her way down the stairs. Soon, they emerged in a dungeon. This was worse – much worse! – than any cave. Darker, damper and with chains hanging from the walls.

They found the Crystal King chained to a wall, his head hanging in misery.

"Oh, dear king!" Aurora rushed over to him and nuzzled him with her velvety nose.

"Aurora!" His eyes lit up. "My love, you came to rescue me!" He caught sight of the girls and Geoffrey sitting in her crown. "Why, whatever happened?" he asked.

But before anyone could answer him, there was a sudden sound of screeching metal. Iron bars slammed to the ground around Aurora and the Crystal King. The two unicorns shook with fear and turned in circles. They were trapped! Emily, Aisha and Geoffrey hung on as Queen Aurora spun. They were feeling dizzy!

"Don't worry," Aisha tried to calm the royal pair, but then they heard a cruel laugh echoing from the top of the stairs.

Selena appeared, her purple eyes flashing.

"*Dear king!*" she mimicked Aurora as she walked down the stairs. "You really need to find something else to say. It's getting boring now."

Emily felt her eyes burn with fury. "Let us go, you meanie!" she cried.

Selena batted her eyelashes. "Absolutely not," she said. "I knew you would come. Silly fools in love are so predictable. And you might be powerful in your valley, Aurora, but my magic cage is strong enough to hold you. So now, you have a simple choice. Make me queen, or be stuck here for ever!"

"Never!" Queen Aurora didn't hesitate, and the girls were so proud of her. The royal unicorn came to stand before her king. "I'll never give up on Enchanted

Valley – or the Crystal King."

"You can't do this!" Heartsong told the evil unicorn.

A smile spread across Selena's face – a wicked kind of smile.
"Oh, but I can." She glanced back at Queen Aurora. "There's nothing you can do, you see. You're trapped! And if you won't give me your kingdom, I'll take it. By force!"

"There is always a way," Emily whispered.

"We promise we'll help," Aisha added.

But despite their words, it was hard to see how they would beat Selena this time.

They held hands and squeezed tight.

Selena threw her head back and laughed, the cold sound echoing off the walls.

"Selena!" The Crystal King pulled at his chains to step towards the bars of the cell.

He bowed, lowering himself in a way the girls had never seen before. Then he took a deep breath and looked up. "If you let Queen Aurora keep her crown, I shall … I shall …" He paused.

Selena drew closer. "Yes?" she asked. Her coat crackled with electricity.

"I'll let you take all my magic," the king said in a rush.

"No!" Queen Aurora gasped.

"You can't!" the girls added.

"Oh, but he can," Selena said, waving a

hoof to quiet them.

Aurora and the Crystal King met each
other's eyes. "You'd do that for me?" she
asked him.

The king glanced back at Selena. Then
he looked at Queen Aurora, whose eyes
brimmed with silver tears. "For you? Of
course."

Aisha and Emily felt a stillness settle
over them. It was as though they'd just

heard one of the most special promises in the world.

Selena took a moment to think. Then she sneered. "No," she snapped. "I don't want your magic." She turned to face Queen Aurora. Her eyes fixed on the glistening circle of diamonds balanced above the queen's ears. "I want the royal crown. And today, finally, I will have it."

Chapter Four
Touching Horns

"No!" the girls cried together.

"You're not getting the crown or the king's magic!" Emily cried.

"Speaking of magic, I've got an idea," Aisha whispered to her friend, crossing her tiny fingers and toes that this would work. "Isn't friendship one of the most

powerful things of all?"

"Yes." Emily nodded.

"And we can see how powerful True Love is," said Aisha. "So, what if Aurora and Heartsong somehow combined their magic? Friendship and Love combined must be the most powerful thing of all."

The girls had meant to whisper to one another and had forgotten that they were sitting right next to the queen's ear, so they were surprised when she answered! "That's a brilliant idea, girls. Heartsong, come here, quickly!"

"What are you doing?" Selena snapped as Heartsong trotted forward and thrust her nose through the bars of the cage.

"Friendship and Love have more power than you know!" Aisha shouted.

Selena snorted. "I don't think so. I don't

have either and I'm *very* powerful."

Aurora and Heartsong touched their noses together.

Selena frowned. "Wait, what are you doing?"

Both their lockets began to glow with a beautiful golden light.

"Stop that now!" Selena screamed, her voice trembling.

And then ... nothing happened.

Selena shrieked with mirth and drummed her hooves. "More power than I know, eh?"

"What if *you* used my True Love locket?" Heartsong suggested to the Crystal King.

Emily clapped her hands together. "Yes! After all, it's Aurora and the Crystal King who are in love and friendship together."

"It's worth a try," Heartsong agreed. She moved closer to the king. In an instant, he nipped the locket from around her throat and slipped it over his head.

"No!" Selena lunged forward with her teeth, but she was too late.

The Crystal King backed away from the bars, towards the wall. Everyone watched and waited – other than Selena, who lunged her head between the bars. But she couldn't reach the king and queen.

The royal unicorns stared deeply into one another's eyes.

"You are my dearest friend," said Queen Aurora as her locket began to glow.

"And you are my truest love," the Crystal King replied, Heartsong's locket

lighting up on his chest.

"Who cares?" Selena screamed. "Love means nothing at all!"

The king and queen brought their horns together. The moment they touched, the bars of the cell melted away like ice-cream in the sun.

The king leapt out, followed by his queen.

Selena spluttered. "But … But …" She gazed around at everyone. "Love can't be that powerful!"

"Yes, it is," Emily told her. She looked at her friend and they slipped their hands together.

"You aren't really surprised?" Aisha asked her. "Didn't you feel it when you wore the True Love locket?"

Selena stomped the ground. Then she let out a huff of disappointment. "Well, yes!" she cried. "But …"

Once again, the girls couldn't help feeling a bit sorry for Selena. She looked so lost.

"Why don't you try being kind and helpful?" Aisha suggested. "Try to make some friends."

"Yes, and not just to be powerful," Emily added. "It feels good. You might find you like it!"

Selena stared at them. She seemed to be turning the idea over in her mind. "OK," she said slowly. "Maybe I will … Is there anything I can do to …" She hesitated on the last word. "Help?" She fetched a small bottle. "This is Bigifying Potion," she explained. "I gave it to my trolls so

they would be extra big and scary. Would
you like some to make you big again?"

"Yes, please," the girls said, then each
took a single drop of the potion. With a
feeling like honey on their tongues, Aisha
and Emily found themselves growing and
growing until suddenly …

"We're full size!" Emily cried.

"Thank you, Selena!" said Aisha.

Selena shuddered. "That felt … weird!"

"You'll get used to it," Emily assured her.

Geoffrey glanced up at them. "What about me?" he asked.

"How big do you want to be?" Aisha asked Geoffrey.

He tipped his head to one side, obviously thinking hard. Then he cried, "Giant sized! You were right, there's no such thing as normal, I just want to be me. And *me* means giant!"

Aisha ruffled his hair with her fingernail. "I agree," she said.

"Me too," said Emily. "But let's go outside first – or you'll crash into the ceiling!"

All of them ran up the steps, out into

the castle courtyard, where Selena gave Geoffrey her potion. His beaming face got further and further away as he shot up, up, up.

Finally, he stopped growing. He smiled down at Selena. "Thank you," he said.

"Erm, you're welcome," Selena said stiffly.

"Can we give you a hug?" Aisha asked the grumpy silver unicorn.

Selena blinked in surprise. "I – er – suppose so."

Aisha and Emily gently slipped their arms around her. She was stiff and crackling with electricity for a moment, but then she relaxed. "Hugging is … nice!" Selena said.

Chapter Five
Royal Unicorn Wedding

The friends flew back over Enchanted Valley, taking in all the sights. They saw their mermaid friends, waving from the sea. There were Ember's chicks, chirping happily together. And at one edge of the valley, they saw Firework Mountain merrily sparking away whilst the dragons

played together in the clouds.

The girls smiled at one another. Families were friends again, Queen Aurora had her true love and it was time to celebrate.

There was only one place to go – Bridal Bower!

They touched down on the cloud among a group of creatures all cheering.

"We're so happy to see you!"

"Your bridal train is ready!"

Lovebirds flew around the clouds, calling out their greetings.

The girls slipped off the unicorns' backs. Heartsong's horn glowed and decorations began to appear from thin air. Garlands of flowers wound around pillars of cloud, pink petals created an aisle from the back of the cloud to the

front, and streamers flew through the air.

Small clouds began to sink to the earth and then rise again, carrying wedding guests. There was Hob, his pointy hat swapped for a top hat. He waved at the girls, settling in on his cloud.

The girls felt the tingle of magic surrounding them and looked down to see their outfits transform. They found themselves wearing dresses in a beautiful shade of pink! The silk was covered in a smattering of sparkles.

Two gnomes appeared on little clouds, holding large bouquets of flowers.

"This one has bluebells for everlasting love," said one gnome, gently pressing the a bouquet into Aisha's hand.

"And this contains lily of the valley so that every day is sweet," said another gnome. He placed a delicate bunch of flowers between Emily's fingers. She dipped her nose into the little bells and drew in their scent.

More and more clouds were arriving, carrying guests and arranging them on either side of an aisle. The pixies from Flowerdew Garden were all dressed in beautiful clothes made of rose petals. Petey the pufflebunny was helping to make the clouds even fluffier and more comfortable to sit on.

The girls heard a gleeful shout and turned to see that Geoffrey was carrying

the mermaids in a giant teacup so that
they could watch the wedding in the sky,
too!

"I really do love flying!" Pearl called.

In all of the bustle, the girls hadn't
noticed Queen Aurora and the Crystal
King appear at the end of the aisle. Quiet
fell and then the lovebirds started to sing.

The queen and king floated slowly
down the aisle together.

Emily and Aisha dipped their hands
into their pockets and pulled out lots of
perfect petals, which they threw over the
royal unicorns like confetti.

This couldn't be more perfect!

Heartsong had taken her place at the
top of the aisle, waiting for the royal
couple to join her. Aurora and the Crystal
King each dipped their heads beneath the

rainbow bower. Heartsong gazed around at the friends who had joined them from all over the valley.

"I declare this ceremony—"

Before Heartsong could finish, there was a flash of lightning and Selena appeared.

"Oh, no!" Emily cried.

"She wouldn't!" Aisha shouted.

They'd all waited so long for this ceremony. Surely it couldn't be ruined now?

But Selena gave a smile. "Sorry I'm late." She held out a gift. It was wrapped in a gold bow.

"I invited her," the Crystal King announced. He turned to look at Selena. "Despite everything that's happened," he said, "I always thought I could see a kind heart."

Aisha and Emily's own hearts swelled. How wise the Crystal King was!

Selena stepped up. "I wanted to show you …" She looked around, as though she didn't want anyone to hear. "To show you … some kindness."

As the last word burst out of her mouth, everyone cheered.

Just then, a glow appeared around the neck of the Crystal King. When it faded away, they saw a locket was hanging there. Inside it, the girls could see a beautiful rainbow.

"The valley has given you the Kindness locket," said Queen Aurora, her eyes shining.

Everyone cheered again. The king was a citizen of the valley now, so he got his own locket!

After that, the ceremony was performed. Beneath the wedding rainbow, Queen Aurora and the Crystal King vowed that their love would keep Enchanted Valley safe for ever. They brought their noses together as Heartsong sent out a song that floated above every creature from Enchanted Valley and bound them together in a promise of love.

Their friends were married and happy. This was all that Aisha and Emily had ever wanted to see. Aurora smiled over to the girls and mouthed "Thank you."

The girls stayed for the party. The food was amazing – Chef Yummytum had made wonderbread sandwiches, with fillings that changed with each bite. There were scones with sweet cream and tartleberry jam. And the most

incredible wedding cake that was five tiers high – each layer a different flavour. They danced to music provided by the leprechaun band. And when the sun finally set, the dragons gave the most thrilling fireworks display – flashing bright colours and shooting sparkling streamers through the air. Ember allowed

her chicks to stay up especially late to
join in the fun.

But it was time to go home, wasn't
it? Aisha and Emily didn't mind if they
slipped away. After all, they'd been
given so many happy goodbyes from
Enchanted Valley.

But as they made their way to the edge

of the dancefloor, there was a little sound behind them. Looking round, they saw Selena standing there.

She reached out a hoof. Dangling from it were two little charms – thunderbolts in a flash of silver! "Thunderbolts for strength. You're the strongest girls I've ever met," she said. "I'm so sorry for all the things I've done. I know this doesn't make up for it … but I want you to have these all the same, for your keyrings."

The girls looked back up at the unicorn's face. "Are you sure?" they asked.

"It would make me … happy." Selena sounded sincere and her face flushed with pleasure.

Aisha and Emily could hardly believe it.

Emily reached out and took the charms. "Thank you," she said shyly.

"You're welcome," Selena said as the two girls linked arms. With a *whoosh!* they were lifted into the air. Then their feet came back to rest in the meadow of flowers.

"I can't believe Selena has changed," Aisha marvelled.

"I know! Now that she is a friend, there won't even be any problems in Enchanted Valley any more!" said Emily.

"Just adventures," Aisha declared.

Emily smiled. "Exactly."

Over their heads, a storm suddenly broke, rain dropping from the grey sky. There was a rumble of thunder and a crash of lightning.

Aisha reached out her elbow.

Emily linked her arm.

Neither of them felt afraid of thunder any more! Then, as quickly as the storm had arrived, the sun came out again. An incredible rainbow appeared above them – just like the one at Aurora's wedding.

"Friends for ever?" Aisha asked.

"Of course!" Emily cried. As though there was any other answer!

The two of them ran beneath the rainbow, clutching each other tight. There really was only one thing better than friendship … unicorns!

The End

Discover how Emily and Aisha's
first adventure began in ...
Dawnblaze
Saves Summer

"I can't believe we're really going to live
here!" said Aisha Khan. She stared up at
her new house, clutching a cardboard box
full of her belongings.

Enchanted Cottage had a thatched
roof, neat little windows and walls the
colour of summer sunshine. The front
garden was bursting with red and blue
flowers. A rose bush grew on either side of
the doorway, spreading over it in a leafy
green and pink canopy.

Aisha's dad threw an arm around her
shoulders. "Home, sweet home!" he said.

"It's perfect," said Aisha, grinning.

The Khans walked up the cobbled path, and Aisha's mum got out the keys. The front door was bright red, with a silver door knocker. It was shaped like a horse's face, with a single silver horn on its forehead.

"A unicorn!" said Aisha's mum, fitting the key in the lock. "I never noticed that before."

The door creaked open, and Aisha raced up the stone stairs to find her bedroom.

The summer sun shone through the window on to the old floorboards. The slanted ceiling had wooden rafters, and there was a soft, cosy bed in the corner. Through the window, Aisha could see the big green lawn of the garden. In the middle was a statue of a magical bird, flying out of a fire. A phoenix, her dad had called it.

She put her box down on the bed. Inside were a tennis racket, swimming goggles, a cricket ball and a big collection of football stickers. Aisha loved sport more than anything.

Just then, the doorbell rang. "I'll get it!" shouted Aisha, and she raced down the stairs.

When she opened the door, she found a girl about her age standing before her. The girl was wearing a stripy T-shirt, shorts and trainers. Her hair hung loose and curly round her shoulders.

"Hi!" said the girl. "I found a football on the road outside." She held it out. "I thought it might be yours."

"Oh, thanks!" said Aisha, taking the ball. "It must have fallen out of the removal lorry."

Read
Dawnblaze Saves Summer
to find out what adventures are in store
for Aisha and Emily!

Also available

Book One:

Dawnblaze Saves Summer

Book Two:

Shimmerbreeze & the Sky Spell

Book Three:

Glitterhoof's Secret Garden

Book Four:

Sparklesplash Meets the Mermaids

Book Five:

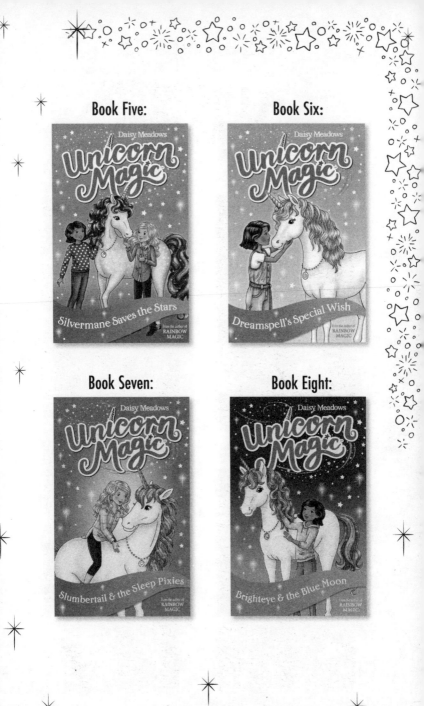

Book Six:

Book Seven:

Book Eight:

Book Nine:

Book Ten:

Book Eleven:

Book Twelve:

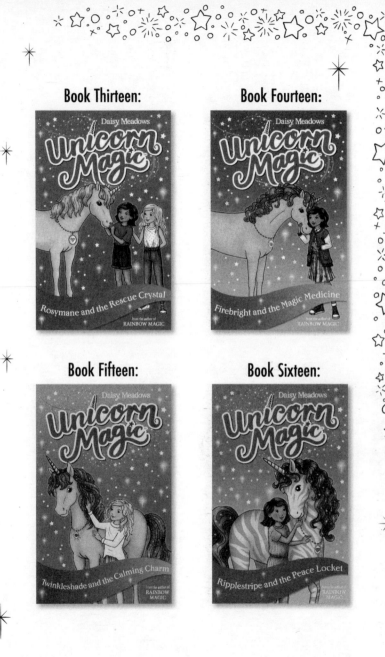

Book Thirteen:

Daisy Meadows

Unicorn Magic

Rosymane and the Rescue Crystal

from the author of
RAINBOW MAGIC

Book Fourteen:

Daisy Meadows

Unicorn Magic

Firebright and the Magic Medicine

from the author of
RAINBOW MAGIC

Book Fifteen:

Daisy Meadows

Unicorn Magic

Twinkleshade and the Calming Charm

from the author of
RAINBOW MAGIC

Book Sixteen:

Daisy Meadows

Unicorn Magic

Ripplestripe and the Peace Locket

from the author of
RAINBOW MAGIC

Special One:

Daisy Meadows

Unicorn Magic

Three stories in one

Snowstar and the Big Freeze

From the author of RAINBOW MAGIC

Special Two:

Daisy Meadows

Unicorn Magic

Three stories in one

Sparklebeam's Holiday Adventure

From the author of RAINBOW MAGIC

Special Three:

Daisy Meadows

Unicorn Magic

Three stories in one

Queen Aurora's Birthday Surprise

From the author of RAINBOW MAGIC

Special Four:

Daisy Meadows

Unicorn Magic

Three stories in one

Sweetblossom and the New Baby

From the author of RAINBOW MAGIC

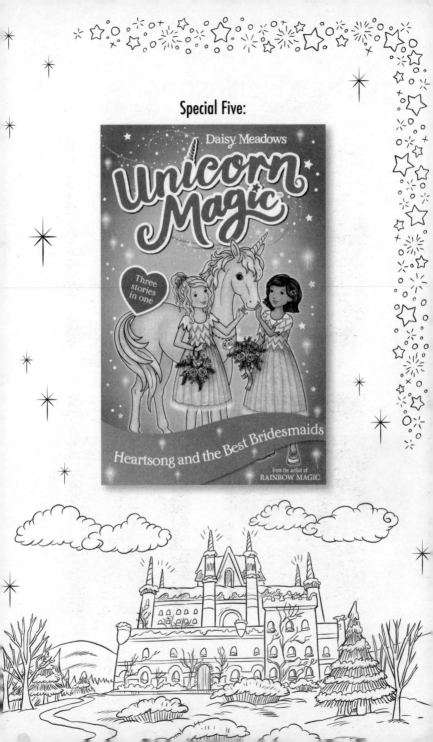

Daisy Meadows

Unicorn Magic™

Three stories in one

Heartsong and the Best Bridesmaids

from the author of
RAINBOW MAGIC

Visit
orchardseriesbooks.co.uk
for

✴ fun activities ✴

✴ exclusive content ✴

✴ book extracts ✴

There's something for everyone!

❀ ORCHARD
SERIES BOOKS